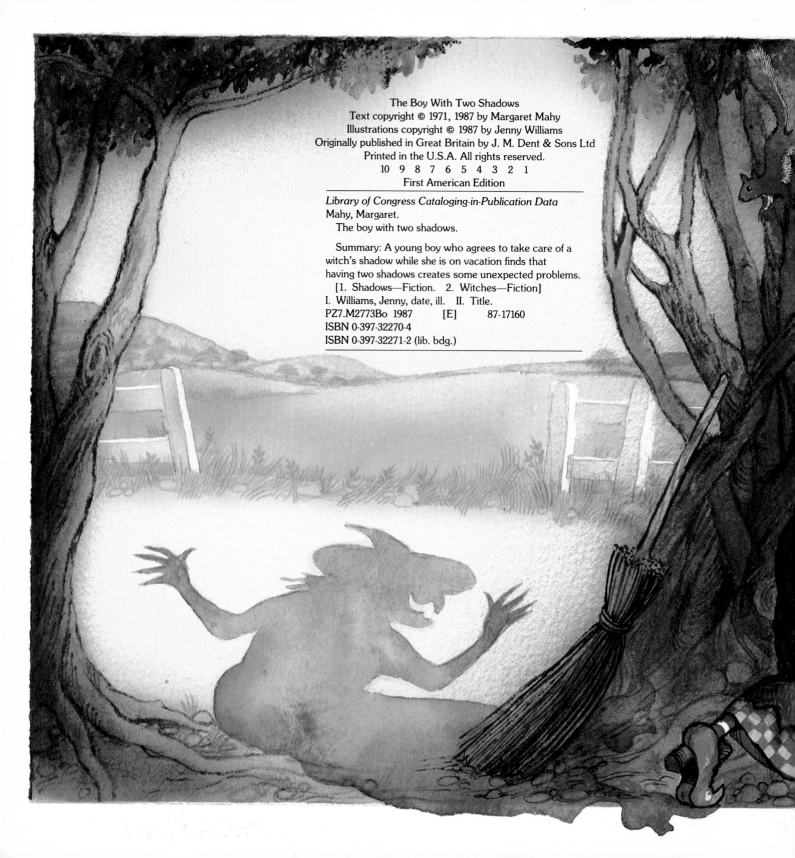

The Boy With Two Shadows
Text copyright © 1971, 1987 by Margaret Mahy
Illustrations copyright © 1987 by Jenny Williams
Originally published in Great Britain by J. M. Dent & Sons Ltd
Printed in the U.S.A. All rights reserved.
10 9 8 7 6 5 4 3 2 1
First American Edition

Library of Congress Cataloging-in-Publication Data
Mahy, Margaret.
    The boy with two shadows.

    Summary: A young boy who agrees to take care of a
witch's shadow while she is on vacation finds that
having two shadows creates some unexpected problems.
    [1. Shadows—Fiction.   2. Witches—Fiction]
I. Williams, Jenny, date, ill.   II. Title.
PZ7.M2773Bo 1987   [E]   87-17160
ISBN 0-397-32270-4
ISBN 0-397-32271-2 (lib. bdg.)

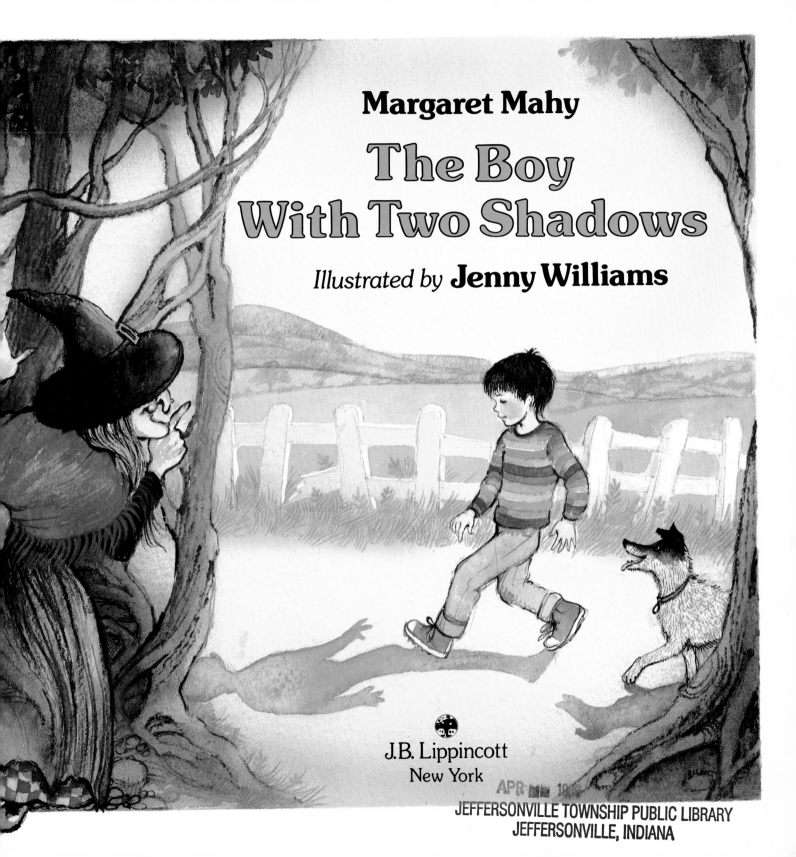

Margaret Mahy

The Boy With Two Shadows

Illustrated by **Jenny Williams**

J.B. Lippincott
New York

There was once a little boy who took great care of his shadow. He was quite a careful little boy with buttons and shoes and all the odd pieces. But most especially he was careful with his shadow, because he knew he had only one, and it had to last him all his life.

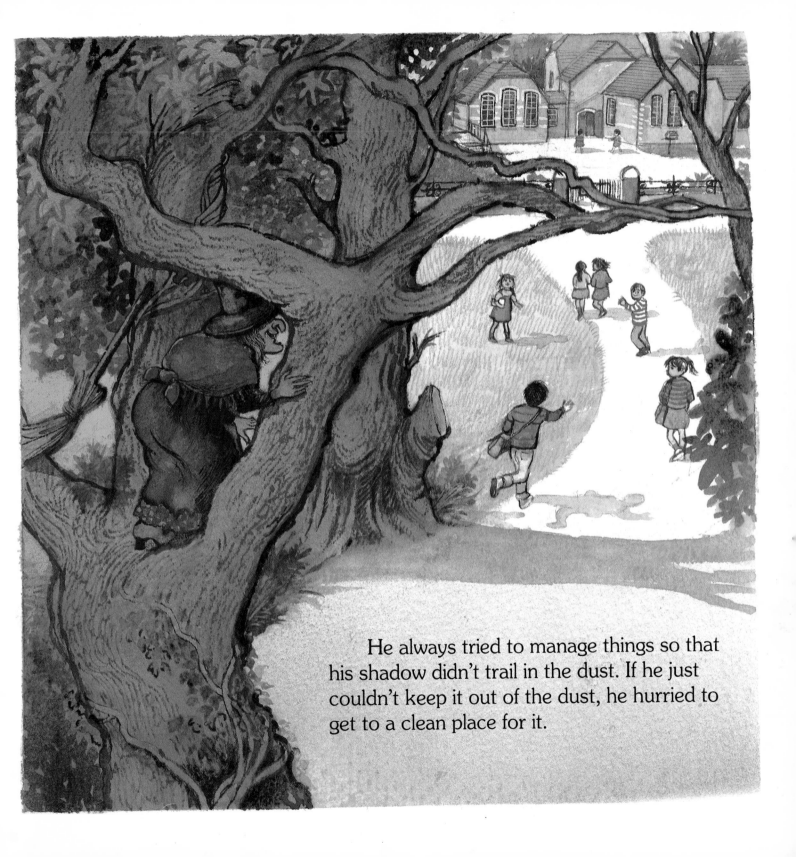

He always tried to manage things so that his shadow didn't trail in the dust. If he just couldn't keep it out of the dust, he hurried to get to a clean place for it.

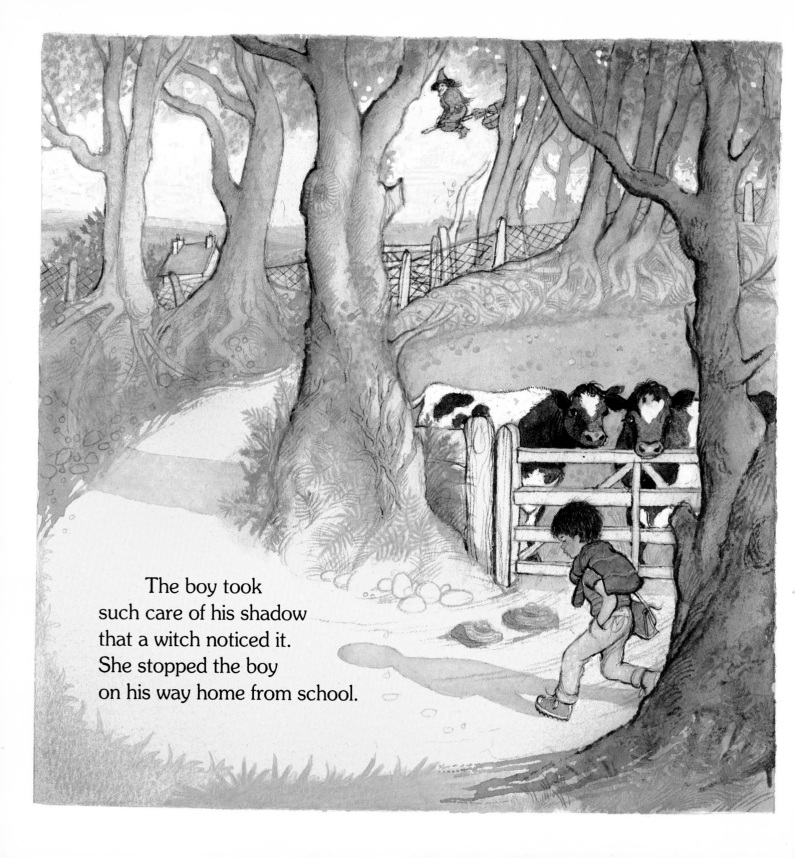

The boy took
such care of his shadow
that a witch noticed it.
She stopped the boy
on his way home from school.

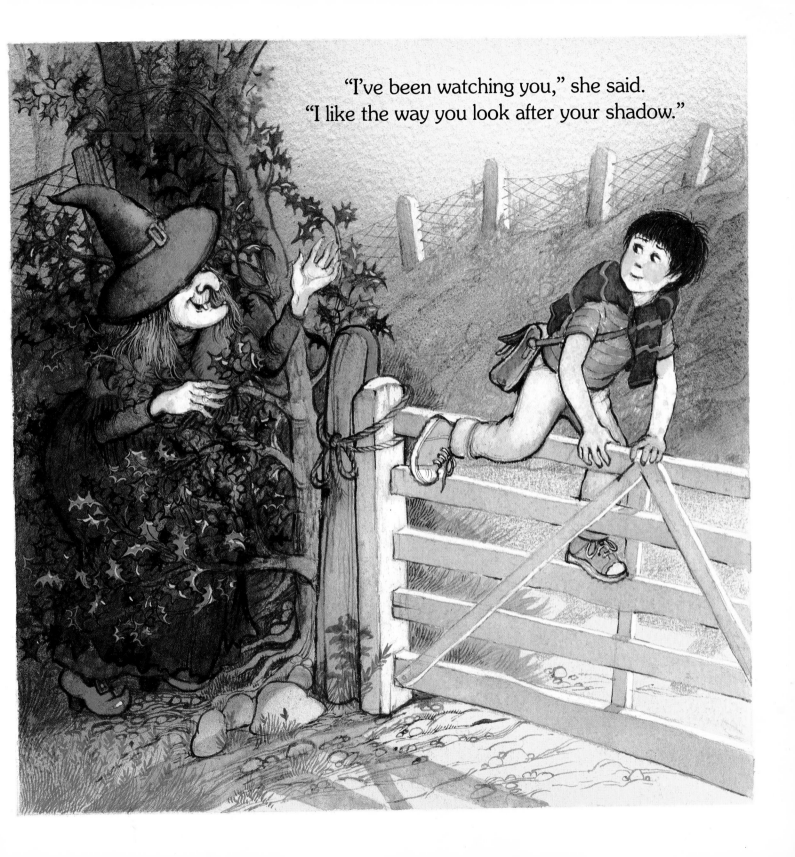

"I've been watching you," she said.
"I like the way you look after your shadow."

"I don't want to wear it out," said the boy. "It's the only one I've got."

"True! True!" said the witch approvingly. "Always look after your shadow! Now, I want someone reliable to look after *my* shadow while I'm away on vacation. You know what a nuisance a shadow can be when you're trying to have a good time."

"My shadow isn't any trouble," said the boy doubtfully.

"I need a good shadow-sitter," the witch declared. "But I'm not going to leave it with just anybody. I've chosen you to take care of it."

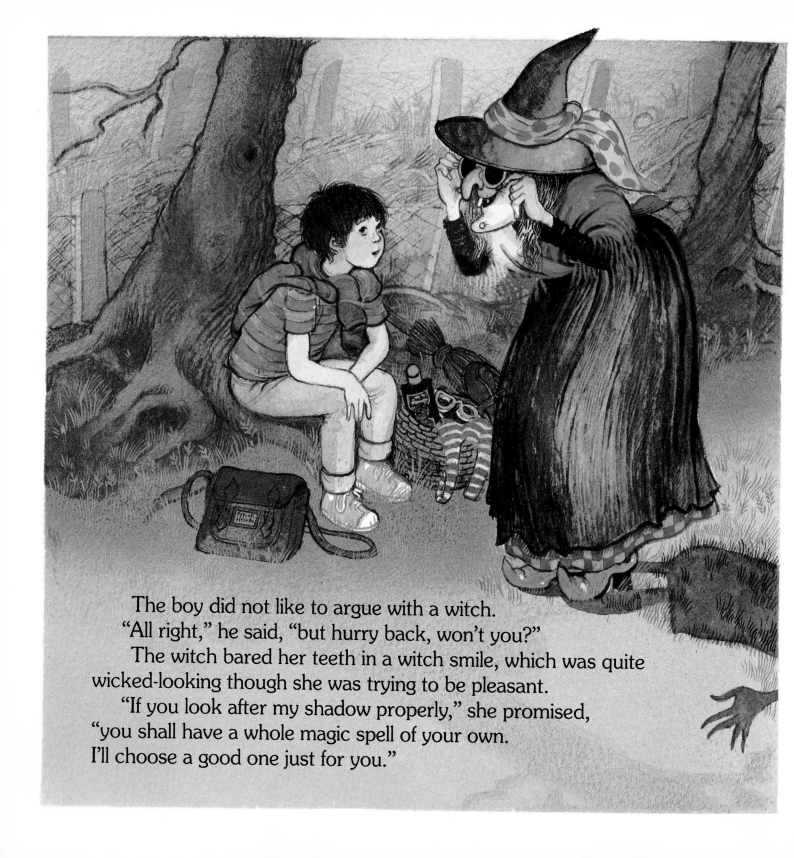

The boy did not like to argue with a witch.

"All right," he said, "but hurry back, won't you?"

The witch bared her teeth in a witch smile, which was quite wicked-looking though she was trying to be pleasant.

"If you look after my shadow properly," she promised, "you shall have a whole magic spell of your own. I'll choose a good one just for you."

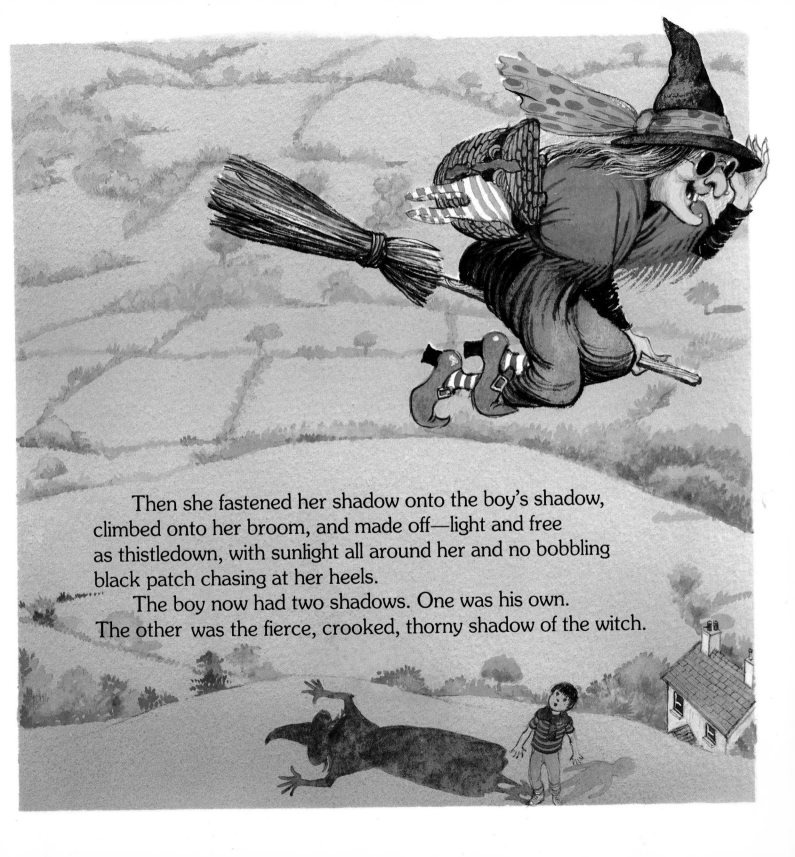

Then she fastened her shadow onto the boy's shadow,
climbed onto her broom, and made off—light and free
as thistledown, with sunlight all around her and no bobbling
black patch chasing at her heels.

    The boy now had two shadows. One was his own.
The other was the fierce, crooked, thorny shadow of the witch.

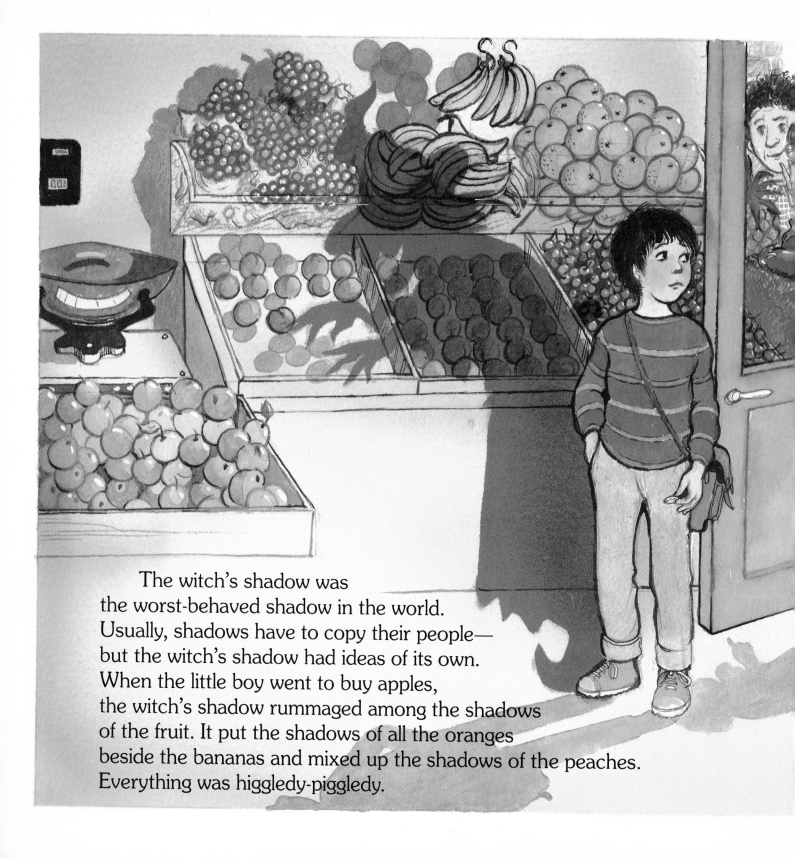

The witch's shadow was
the worst-behaved shadow in the world.
Usually, shadows have to copy their people—
but the witch's shadow had ideas of its own.
When the little boy went to buy apples,
the witch's shadow rummaged among the shadows
of the fruit. It put the shadows of all the oranges
beside the bananas and mixed up the shadows of the peaches.
Everything was higgledy-piggledy.

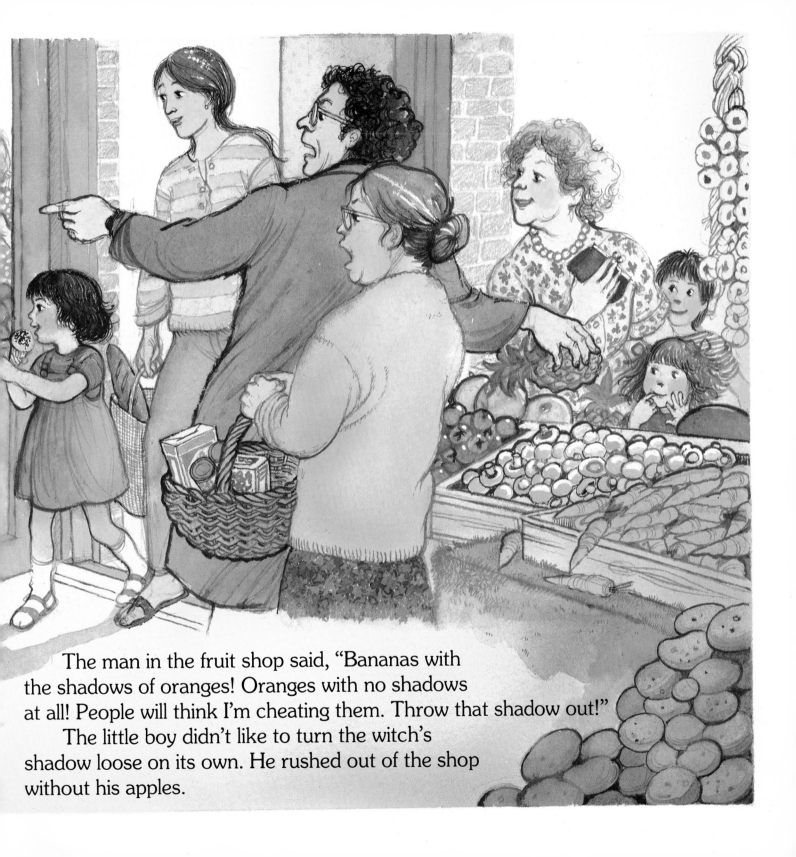

The man in the fruit shop said, "Bananas with the shadows of oranges! Oranges with no shadows at all! People will think I'm cheating them. Throw that shadow out!"

The little boy didn't like to turn the witch's shadow loose on its own. He rushed out of the shop without his apples.

At home, during tea, the witch's shadow stretched itself long and leaped all over the wall. It took the shadow from the clock, and the clock stopped. Then it terrified the parrot into fits, and pulled the shadow tail of the dog's shadow. "Really!" said the little boy's mother. "That wicked shadow is making me spill my tea and cut the cake crooked. Couldn't you keep it outside?"

The boy didn't
want his mother to
spill her tea, but he
was determined to
look after the witch's shadow.
From then on he had his tea in the kitchen on his own.

He became so clever at keeping the witch's shadow from getting into mischief and wickedness that at last it couldn't find anything wicked to do.

Naturally this made it very cross.

Suddenly it thought of something very, very mean—so mean that you would think even a witch's shadow would be ashamed. It started teasing and terrifying the little boy's *own* shadow. It was terrible to see. The boy's shadow had always been treated kindly. It did not know what to do now about this new, fierce thing that pushed it out of gardens and gutters, that pinched it, prodded it, poked it—treading on its heels as they hurried down the road.

One day the boy's shadow could bear this no longer. In broad daylight the boy, going home to lunch, saw his two shadows — short and squat — running beside him. The witch's shadow nipped his own shadow with her long witch fingernails. It gave a great bound and broke free from his feet. Away, away it flew on its own, leaping silently, tumbling off like a bit of wastepaper blown by a secret wind.

Then it was gone. The little boy ran after it, but it was nowhere to be seen. He stood still. He listened. The warm summer afternoon was so quiet, he could hear the witch shadow laughing — or rather, he heard the echo of laughing (because, as you know, an echo is the shadow of sound, and sometimes the sound of a shadow).

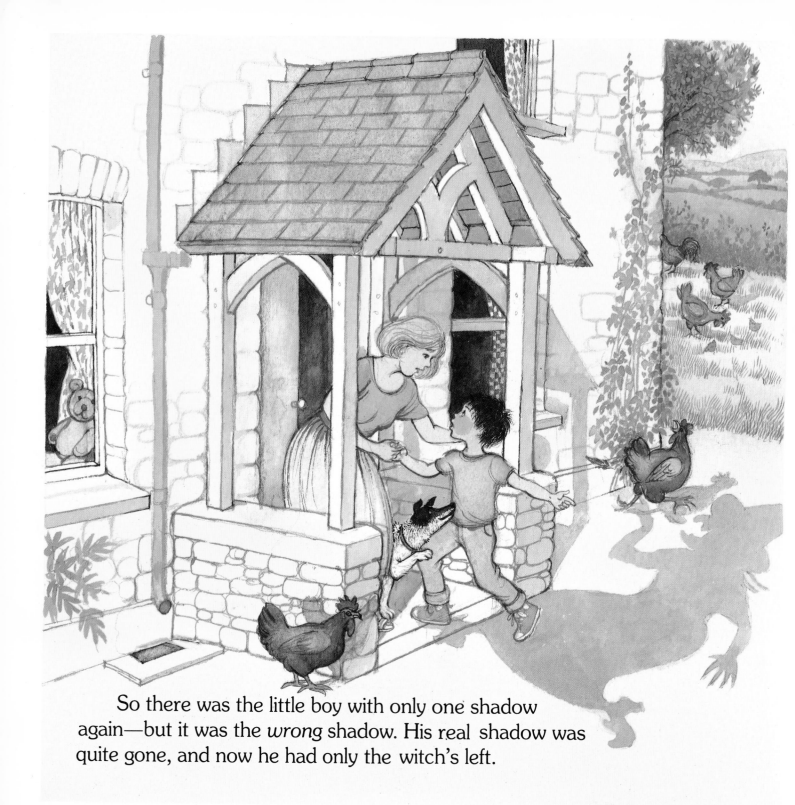

So there was the little boy with only one shadow
again—but it was the *wrong* shadow. His real shadow was
quite gone, and now he had only the witch's left.

It was more like having a thorn bush at his heels than a proper shadow—a thorn bush that could pull faces, too. People stared and pointed, and shrank away. As for the boy, he felt sad and lonely without his own shadow. He tried to enjoy having the witch's shadow, but it was like trying to pet a wild wolf or thistle.

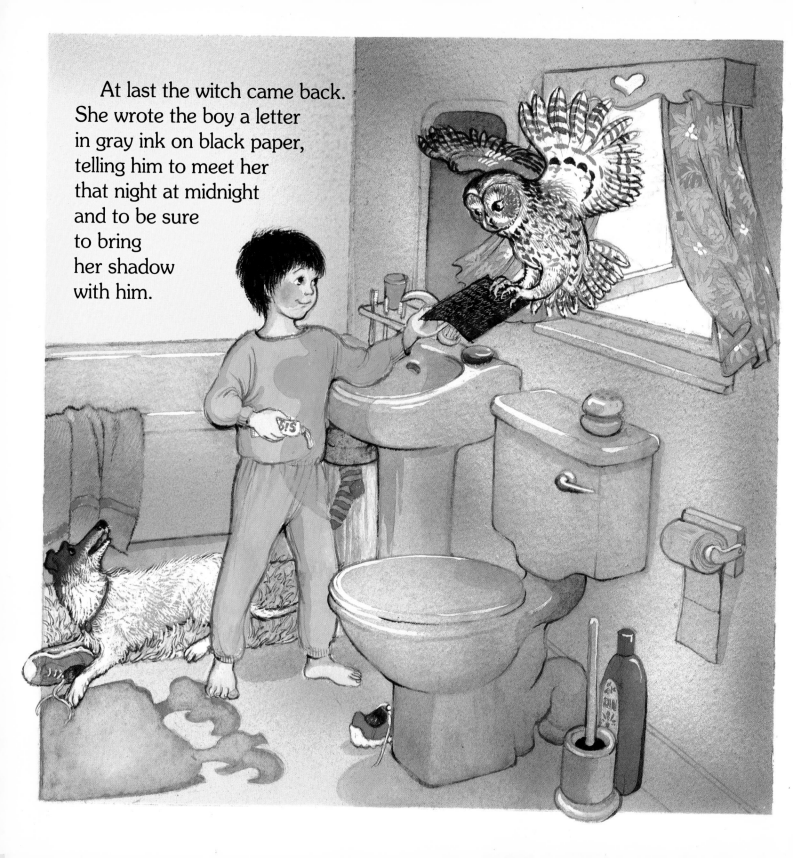

At last the witch came back.
She wrote the boy a letter
in gray ink on black paper,
telling him to meet her
that night at midnight
and to be sure
to bring
her shadow
with him.

(Thank goodness it was a bright moonlit night, or it might have been extremely difficult to find that wretched shadow, which sometimes hid away from him.)

"Aha!" said the witch when she saw it, and
she whisked it back in half a minute less than
no time—or even faster.

"And here's your spell," she said. "Defrost it, bake it, and then eat it."
The spell was written on a quick-frozen sausage roll.

"What will it do?" asked the boy.
"Turn you into a camel," said the witch. "A white racing camel—or
a Bactrian, or any sort of camel you like—but just for an hour or two."

The little boy didn't really want to turn himself into a camel—even for an hour or two. He wanted his own shadow back again.

"Your fierce shadow has chased mine away," he told the witch sternly.

The witch snickered a bit in a witchlike fashion.

"Well, my dear," she said, "you can't expect everything to be easy, you know. Anyhow, I feel I've paid you handsomely for your trouble. Run off home now."

And off she went, taking her shadow with her. It didn't even bother to wave good-bye.

The boy went home shadowless through a moonlit world of shadows. Trees had shadows. Fence posts had shadows. Sleeping cows had sleeping shadows around them. The boy felt very lonely.

But as he walked home, something dark and mysterious came to meet him. It copied everything he did. He took a step and *it* took a step. He waved, and it waved back. Softly and shyly, as if it were ashamed of itself, his own shadow sidled toward him. It had been hiding among other shadows, keeping an eye on him. Now it slipped along toe to toe with him just as it had always done.

The little boy thought for a moment. The wicked witch shadow was gone. He could turn into any sort of camel he liked—and a mischievous camel could have a lot of fun at the school fancy-dress ball—just for an hour or two. Best of all, he had his own shadow back again.

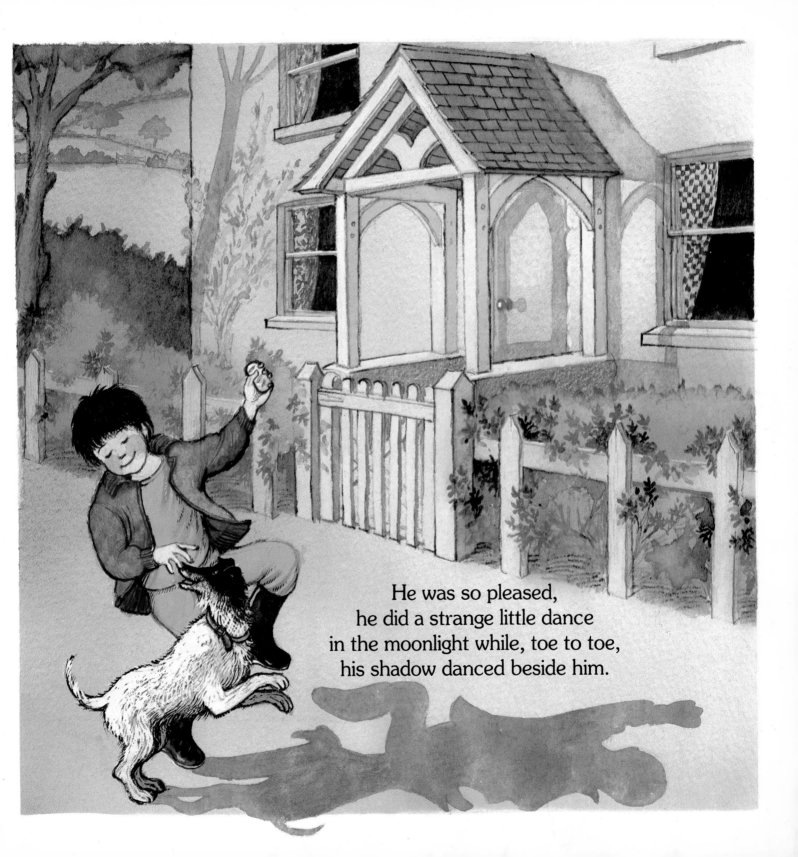

He was so pleased,
he did a strange little dance
in the moonlight while, toe to toe,
his shadow danced beside him.

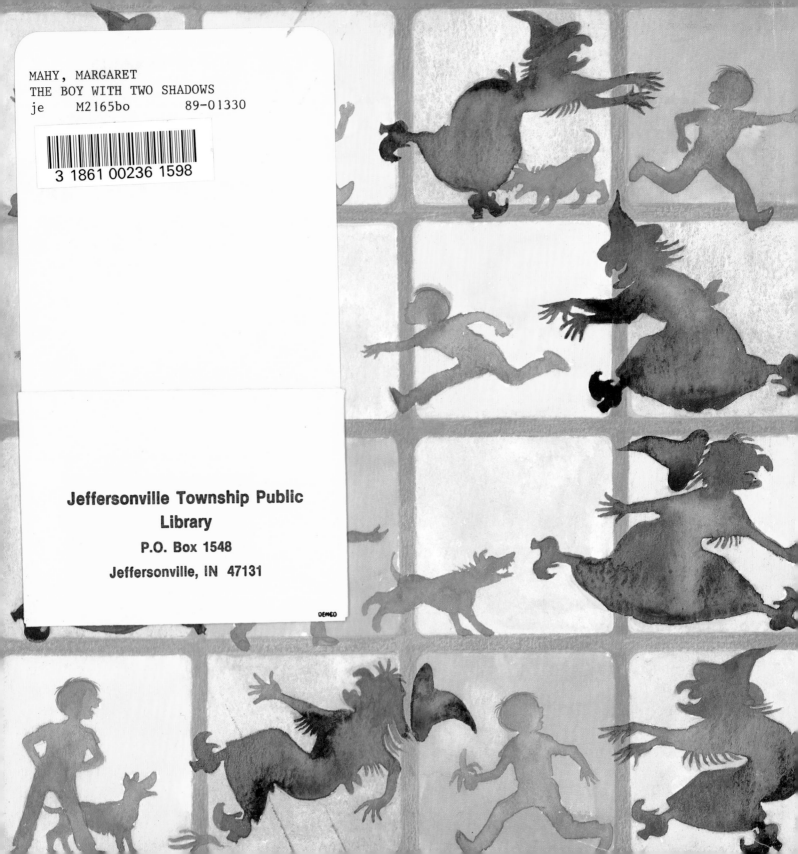